ISBN 0-86163-495-0 (cased)
ISBN 0-86163-826-3 (limp)

Copyright © 1991 Award Publications Limited

First published 1991 (cased edition)
First published 1996 (limp edition)

Published by Award Publications Limited,
1st Floor, 27 Longford Street,
London, NW1 3DZ

Printed in Belgium

JACK and the BEANSTALK

Illustrated by Rene Cloke

To Cameron

AWARD PUBLICATIONS

Jack and his mother kept a cow
named Daisy and ten hens in the
garden of their little cottage.

A wicked giant had killed Jack's
father and taken all his money
but they had plenty of milk,
butter and eggs to eat and to sell.

One night, a fox crept into the hen-house, killed all the hens and ran off with them.

"Oh dear!" cried Jack's mother. "We shall have no eggs to sell so we cannot buy bread or clothes."

They decided that Jack must take Daisy to market and sell her.

"Be sure you get a good price for her," said his mother, "she is a fine cow."

Jack went off to the market very sadly leading poor Daisy. On his way he met a strange looking man.

"I will give you something valuable for that cow," said the stranger and he showed Jack a handful of coloured beans.

"Plant those, my lad," he said, "and you will make a fortune."
"How wonderful!" said Jack and he handed the cow to the strange man.

Jack's mother was very angry when
she saw the beans.

"We can't live on those!" she cried
and threw them out of the window
into the garden.

When Jack looked out of his window
the next morning he had a great shock.
A huge beanstalk was growing in the
garden, so high that he could not see
the top.

"Look, mother!" he cried.
"The beans *were* magic!"
Jack's mother was greatly
surprised and very frightened
when Jack said he would climb the
beanstalk and find his fortune at the top.

"Don't be afraid," cried Jack, "we shall
soon be very rich!"

It was a long,
long way to climb
for the beanstalk
twisted around and
around and Jack could
see nothing but green
leaves, beans and red
flowers.

At last he came to
the top and looked along
a winding road.

There was a castle
ahead of him
and Jack decided
to go and ask who
lived there and
what strange country
he had reached.

When he arrived at the castle
he could see no one about so
he went to the great door and
knocked on the knocker.

"Who lives here?" he shouted.

Such a big woman opened
the door that Jack nearly
fell over in surprise.

"And who may you be?" she
asked.

"I've climbed the beanstalk to
seek my fortune," answered Jack,
"and I'm very hungry."

"You may come in and have some bread and cheese," said the big woman, "but beware of my husband when he comes home, for he will be ready for *his* dinner."

Jack enjoyed his meal, but as he finished it, he heard the footsteps of the giant.

"Quick!" whispered the giant's wife. "Hide in the oven!" She shut Jack in the oven as the giant came in.

"Fee-fi-fo-fum!" he cried. "I smell the blood of an Englishman.
Be he alive or be he dead –
I'll grind his bones to make my bread!"

But his wife told him the smell was
of the huge dinner of three sheep
that she was roasting.

After his dinner, the giant sat
down to count his money bags, but
he soon grew tired and fell asleep.

Jack crept out and, snatching one of the money bags, he ran from the castle and down the road.

Clutching the heavy bag, he climbed down the beanstalk.

"Look, Mother!" he cried. "Here is our fortune; that was the giant who killed my father and took his money!"

They were now able to buy back the cow, Daisy, and some more hens and some good clothes.

Jack soon began to think
again about the great castle
at the top of the beanstalk.

He wondered what treasures
the giant kept there.

I must climb up again, he
decided.

The giant's wife did not
recognise him as he was wearing
a fine new suit.

"The last boy who came here
ran off with a bag of money,"
she told him as she gave him
a bowl of soup.

Jack hid in the oven when
the giant came home to his dinner.

He called for his magic hen and
to Jack's astonishment the hen laid
a golden egg when the giant called "Lay!"

When the giant fell asleep, Jack seized the hen and rushed from the castle.

"Cackle, cackle!" cried the hen and the giant and his wife chased after Jack but he was too quick for them and they did not see which way he went.

"Don't go again," his mother begged him.

"Just one more adventure," pleaded Jack. This time the giant called for his harp and Jack heard it play lovely music by itself.

As soon as the giant slept, Jack ran off with the harp.

"Master! Master!" cried the harp and the giant woke up.

Jack scrambled down
the beanstalk with
the giant climbing
after him.

"Bring me the axe, Mother!"
called Jack.

With a mighty blow of the axe, Jack chopped down the beanstalk and down tumbled the giant, head over heels and never got up again.

So Jack and his mother lived
happily with the cow, Daisy and
the hens. They had as much
money as they could want and the
magic harp to play beautiful music
whenever it was asked.